Missouri

Arkansas

Tennessee

Mississippi

Alabama

FEB - 2005

Going North

JANICE N. HARRINGTON

PICTURES BY

JEROME LAGARRIGUE

MELANIE KROUPA BOOKS

FARRAR, STRAUS AND GIROUX   NEW YORK

To my mother, Anna I. Day, with special thanks to Janice Del Negro
—J.N.H.

To Virginia Barlow
—J.L.

Copyright © 2004 by Janice N. Harrington
Illustrations copyright © 2004 by Jerome Lagarrigue
All rights reserved
Distributed in Canada by Douglas & McIntyre Publishing Group
Printed and bound in the United States of America by Berryville Graphics
Designed by Jennifer Browne
First edition, 2004
10 9 8 7 6 5 4 3

www.fsgkidsbooks.com

Library of Congress Cataloging-in-Publication Data
Harrington, Janice N..
    Going north / by Janice N. Harrington ; pictures by Jerome Lagarrigue.— 1st ed.
      p. cm.
    Summary: A young African American girl and her family leave their home in Alabama
and head for Lincoln, Nebraska, where they hope to escape segregation and find a better life.
    ISBN-13: 978-0-374-32681-4
    ISBN-10: 0-374-32681-9
    [1. Moving, Household—Fiction.   2. African Americans—Fiction.   3. Race
relations—Fiction.   4. Southern States—20th century—Fiction.]   I. Lagarrigue, Jerome, ill.
II. Title.

PZ7.H23815 Go 2004
[E]—dc21

2002032207

At Big Mama's house
everyone sits around the supper table
talking about life up North. Everyone talks
and talks about how much better the North is,
how Daddy can find a good job there,
and how I can go to a better school.
But isn't it good here?
Can't we just stay?

I don't want to go.
I want to stay in Big Mama's kitchen,
helping her churn the butter up-down,
up-down, *taw-whomp, taw-whomp,*
swapping stories, and watching Big Mama
knife-scrape a sweet potato, dragging
its blade across orange pulp
and sharing a sweet treat.

"I don't want to go," I tell Big Mama.
But Going-North Day hurries to our door
like it's tired of our slowpokey ways.

Everybody comes to say goodbye:
uncles, aunts, cousins too,
Brother, Baby Sister, and me
picked up, put down, passed around,
and tickle-twirled all over the place.
Everyone says, "Goodbye, we'll miss you."

I slip off my shoes and push my feet
into the rusty sand. I wish my toes were roots.
I'd grow into a pin oak and never go away.
Would they let me stay if I were a tree?

Car loaded, everything packed,
goodbyes said. We're almost ready.

I run to Big Mama one last time.
She hugs me tight.
"Take care of your mama," she says.
"Be a good girl, Jessie. Y'all take care."

"Bye-bye, Big Mama!"
"Bye-bye!"

Our station wagon pulls away, banana bright,
rolling, rolling down a red dirt hill.

We're going North.

"Goodbye, Big Mama."
"Goodbye, Popalop."
We're going North, leaving
Alabama far behind.

We're going North
in a yellow station wagon,
Mama, Daddy,
Brother, Baby Sister,
and me looking out,
looking at the world going by,
red sand and cotton fields,
pines marking the sky
like black crayons,
listening to the tires
make a road-drum, a road-beat:

good
    luck

good
    luck

good
    luck

Kudzu vines covering everything,
kudzu leaves like big green hands
clapping, clapping and waving to us.
Brother pointing at all he sees,
Baby Sister bouncing on my lap, lap, lap,
and Mama helping Daddy, checking the map.
Daddy's eye steady on the road,
then studying the gas gauge, measuring the miles.

Going by an old man selling peaches,
going by tin roofs, front porches, going by
brown girls jumping rope, rope, rope,
brown legs flying high.
Maybe later they'll play Little Sally Walker.

Do they play Little Sally Walker in the North?
Do they play ring games?
Oh, wipe your weepin' eye,
Oh, wipe your weepin' eye.

Cotton fields stretch out,
brown shoulders dragging croaker sacks,
brown fingers picking cotton under a red pepper sun.

We're going on.
Cotton fields getting smaller, going by.
Even the people getting smaller, going by.
Mississippi on and on.
Mississippi, Mississippi going by.

"Lunchtime, are you hungry?"
Picnic basket and paper plates,
Big Mama's tea cakes,
potato salad and lemonade,
cold chicken and corn bread.

The car smells like chicken.
Our fingers taste salty sweet.
We're riding in a lemonade car,
a yellow station wagon, heading North.

Sitting in the back, I see a big world.
I hear the tires bumping, beating out

good
    bye

good
    bye

good
    bye

Down the road and the baby's crying.
Mama's singing, hush, hush.
Brother's fussing, hush, hush.
Daddy's watching the gas gauge.
"It's running out, child, running out."

"Where will we go, Daddy? Where will we go?"
"Hush now, quiet now, Daddy's got to drive."
Gas gauge getting low, getting low.

Can't stop just anywhere.
Only the Negro stations,
only the Negro stores.

Mama's praying, sees another town up ahead.
Daddy's searching, looking out,
holding the wheel knuckle-tight.
Even Brother seems to know.
Baby's quiet, won't even cry.

Will we make it?
Will this place serve Negroes?
Gas gauge says

almost
gone

almost

gone

Joe's Gas, up ahead,
plenty of Negro faces,
plenty of Negro smiles.
Daddy breathes a heavy sigh.
Mama hugs Baby Sister
tight, tight, tight.
Brother wants candy.
Me too! Me too!

Joe comes smelling like gasoline
and fills our tank.
"Y'all cutting it close," he says.
Daddy sighs and shakes his head.

We're on the road again, moving fast,
car filled with gasoline,
Brother wearing a chocolate bar.
Mama's hand on Daddy's shoulder.
Long road, but we're moving fast, moving fast.

I think about Daddy's hands all knuckle-tight.
I think about Mama's prayer
and the gas gauge running out.
Maybe the North *will* be better—

may
 be

may
 be

may
 be

Arkansas, now, and it's getting late.
Still a long way to go.

Sister's asleep on Mama's lap,
Brother's curled up puppy-tight,
but I'm looking out.

Ink-black, soot-black, skillet-black night.
The road hurtling by.
Mama and Daddy talking in low voices.

Outside I see stars and the Big Dipper.
We're following the Big Dipper, going North.

More stars than I can count,
blue and white like dashboard lights.
They're gleaming in and I'm looking out.

Sleepy now. Nighttime rolling by.
The road whispers, the tires mumble

good
  night

good
  night

good
  night

Daybreak, and Daddy beside the road,
tired, stretching,
seeing the way ahead,
all of us waking up.

Missouri stone, Missouri hills,
are we there yet?

Almost there.
We're leaving Dixie,
almost there.
"Will I like the North?"
"Honey, I don't know."

The road-drums, the road-beats

don't know

    don't know

        don't know

Are we there yet?
Almost there.
Will we be there soon?
Almost there.

And then—

Welcome to Nebraska,
the sign says.

This is it?
No more cotton fields,
no more red sand,
no more June bugs on a cotton string.

Instead, I see black dirt everywhere,
black magic, North magic.
Nebraska rolling by on a grassy rug.

Brother presses his nose
against the window. Baby Sister
sniffle-sighs, sniffle-sighs.
Mama soothes us with her smile.
But I just keep staring out,
looking and looking.

Until finally I see

Lin-coln
Lin-coln
Lincoln, Nebraska!

"We're here now," Daddy says.
"Going to start a brand-new life.
We're going to be pioneers."

Daddy, Mama,
Brother, Baby Sister, and me,
all pioneers, all looking out,
hearing a heart-drum

be
        brave
be
        brave

Be brave. We're together.
Pioneers.

A Note from the Author

My family moved from Vernon, Alabama, to Lincoln, Nebraska, during the summer of 1964. Like other African Americans, my parents moved North to find good jobs and better schools for their children and to escape segregation. Especially in the South, African Americans couldn't live in the same neighborhoods, attend the same schools, or even ride in the same sections of trains or buses as white Americans. Traveling through the South was difficult and even dangerous for African American families. They often couldn't find motels, gas stations, or restaurants that would serve them or treat them fairly. Things that white Americans could take for granted—drinking from a water fountain, going to the rest room, or sitting in a park—were challenges for Negro families. Which drinking fountain could they use? Where could they sit? Will this place serve Negroes?

Leaders such as Dr. Martin Luther King, Jr., and thousands of men, women, and children fought hard to change the laws and end segregation. Gradually, the laws that kept Americans separate began to change.

Years later, I saw that my family and other African American families were like the pioneers that settled the American West. Like those pioneers, we left all we knew, faced dangers, and started new lives, hoping for a better future.